STARS
ON THE
COURT

by Paul Ladewski

SCHOLASTIC INC.

New York   Toronto   London   Auckland   Sydney
Mexico City   New Delhi   Hong Kong   Buenos Aires

Photos:

Front cover (left to right): Sam Forencich; D. Clark Evans; Brian Babineau

Back cover (left to right): Glenn James; Glenn James; Fernando Medina

Interior: (4) Andrew D. Bernstein ; (10) Ned Dishman; (13, 14) Allen Einstein; (15) David Liam Kyle; (5 (top), 16, 18 (left)) Barry Gossage; (17) D. Lippitt/Einstein; (6, 19, 20, 21, 23) Glenn James; (22) Ronald Martinez ; (24) D. Clarke Evans; (5 (bottom), 18 (right), 25, 26) Nathaniel S. Butler; (11, 12, 27, 29, 32) Fernando Median; (7, 8, 9, 28) Brian Babineau; (5 (middle), 31) Garrett Ellwood

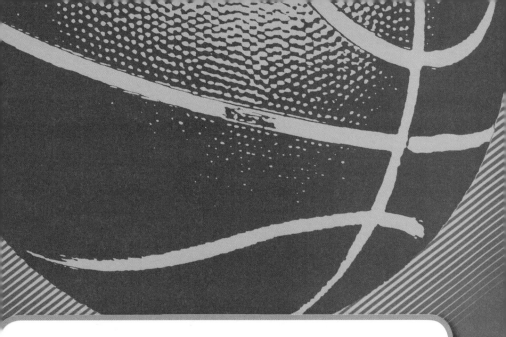

Contents

INTRODUCTION

The best NBA players come in all shapes and sizes.

In the backcourt, there are superquick guards such as Steve Nash, Tony Parker, and Chris Paul. They are like quarterbacks on the court, guys who handle the ball, pass it to open teammates, and run the show.

On the wings, there are do-it-alls such as Carmelo Anthony, Kevin Garnett, LeBron James, Tracy McGrady, and Dirk Nowitzki. They can do more things than a Swiss Army knife—pull down rebounds, take the ball to the bucket, shoot mid-range shots, maybe even step out and hoist a three-pointer once in awhile.

And close to the basket, there are big bodies such as Tim Duncan and Dwight Howard. They're the tall timber who are expected to grab rebounds and block shots at one end, and score from close range at the other.

The best NBA players also come from different cities and even countries.

Carmelo, Chris, Dwight, LeBron, Kevin, and Tracy have hometowns in the United States. Dirk, Steve, Tim, and Tony were born and raised in other parts of the world.

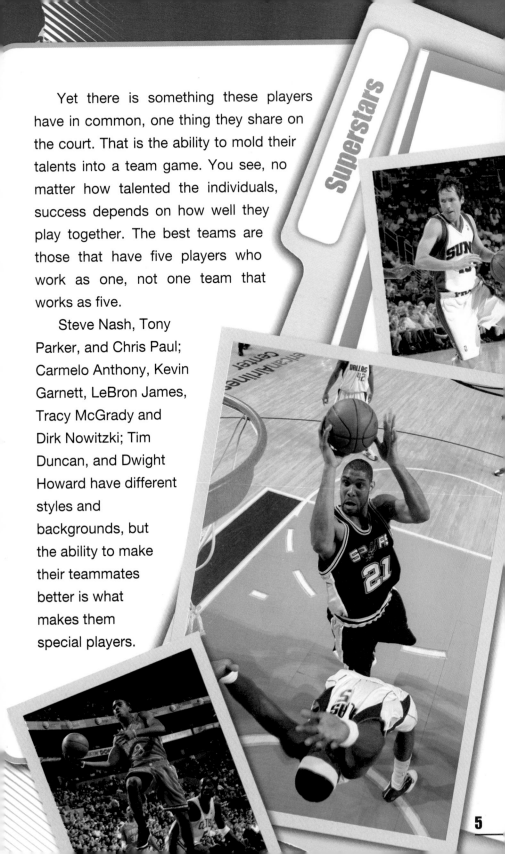

Yet there is something these players have in common, one thing they share on the court. That is the ability to mold their talents into a team game. You see, no matter how talented the individuals, success depends on how well they play together. The best teams are those that have five players who work as one, not one team that works as five.

Steve Nash, Tony Parker, and Chris Paul; Carmelo Anthony, Kevin Garnett, LeBron James, Tracy McGrady and Dirk Nowitzki; Tim Duncan, and Dwight Howard have different styles and backgrounds, but the ability to make their teammates better is what makes them special players.

When it comes to basketball, you name it and Kevin Garnett probably has done it in his NBA career.

Summer Olympics? Been there. Most Valuab[le] Player? Done that. All-Star Game? Been there. Leagu[e] leader in points and rebounds? Done that, too.

Kevin does have something left on his to-do list, the one thing th[at] would make his career a complete success.

"To win a championship, I'd give whatever," say[s] Kevin, who is known as "K.G." and "The Big Ticket."

While Kevin played on some very good Minnesot[a] Timberwolves teams in his career, none of them wer[e] talented enough to capture the grand prize. But tha[t] changed after the 2006–2007 season, when the Timberwolves traded him in one of the biggest deals ever. The Boston Celtics gave up five players and a pair of first-round draft picks to get him!

A few days earlier, guard Ray Allen came to Boston, too. The combination of Paul Pierce, along with newcomers Ray and Kevin gave the Celtics not one, not two, but three All-Star players.

"I'll bring what I bring to the table, but it's good to know you have two guys with the experience and know-how in big games," says Kevin, one of the most popular players in the league.

Many experts believe Kevin is as close to the perfect basketball player as humanly possible. At 6-foot-11, he has the size to play close to the

basket. At the same time, his 253-pound body is so flexible and his arms are so long that Kevin is sort of like Gumby in basketball shorts.

Kevin can dribble, shoot, and defend so well for his size that he doesn't have a position, really. While he usually plays one of the forward spots, K.G. can also move to center and sometimes even guard.

As gifted as Kevin is as an athlete, his attitude separates him from many of the rest. A leader on the court, he is very enthusiastic and quick to offer encouragement to his teammates.

As Kevin says, "I truly don't care how many points I score. I get far more satisfaction out of doing the other things that make us winners."

Do you believe in Magic?

Well, as long as Dwight Howard is around, then it would a good idea to believe that the Orlando Magic could one day a championship team.

Championship teams have to be able to protect their basket, a Dwight Howard has the kind of rebounding skills that just might make t Orlando Magic a championship team someday.

"I just want to get out there and help my team win," says Dwig "We're a playoff team, but talent will only take you so far. As a team, we need to get a little hungrier."

Dwight is 6'11", but he leaps like somebody who is a lot shorter. He can rise up nearly 40 inches off the ground, which is quite unusual for somebody who weighs 265 pounds.

Yet, as Dwight can tell you, it takes more than jumping to be an effective rebounder. He also has to be in the right

position to grab the ball—and he has to want it more than his opponen does. Dwight does these things as well as or better than any big mar around.

Dwight has developed into a 20-points-per-game scorer, too. If he gets the ball close to the basket, then look out below! In the 2005–2006 and 2006–2007 seasons, Dwight (who's sometimes called "Thunder") had

the most dunks in the league. He won the 2008 Sprite Slam Dunk— and even put on a Superman cape before he threw one down.

But what if Dwight is a bit farther away from the bucket? No problem. He can pull a jump hook out of his bag.

Dwight is very active off the court as well. Along with his parents, Dwight started the Dwight Howard Foundation, which offers scholarships to students and organizes summer basketball camps for girls and boys. He is also involved in the NBA Read to Achieve program.

Still only 23 years old, Dwight has plenty of time to grow on and off the court. He wants to improve his ability to pass, to handle the ball, and to shoot free throws.

"I got some work to do," says Dwight, a true believer. "We've got some time. This will be a good team. We've just got to get it all together."

Trying to pick the best basketball player is sort of like trying to choose your favorite candy.

Red licorice? Chocolate kisses? Gummies? Peanut butter cups?

Kobe Bryant? Tim Duncan? Kevin Garnett? LeBron James?

See, it's not easy to decide, is it?

But after what Cleveland Cavaliers superstar LeBron James did in the 2008 All-Star Game, he certainly picked up a few more votes as the best in the world.

With the score tied in the final minute, LeBron swiped a pass at one end of the court. Then the 23-year-old forward dunked the ball over a pair of defenders at the opposite side of the court. The East team went wild—and went on to win the game.

The man called "King James" was crowned Most Valuable Player for the second time in the last three seasons. He finished with 27 points, nine assists, and eight rebounds.

"There is a lot of pressure put on me, but I don't put a lot of pressure on myself," says LeBron, who was born in Akron, Ohio. "I feel if I play my game, it will take care of itself."

Anybody who saw King James in the 2007 playoffs wasn't surprised to see him take over the game in the final minute.

In Game 5 versus the Detroit Pistons, LeBron scored a total of 48 points for the Cavaliers. And with 2.2 seconds on the clock in double overtime, his layup decided the game!

"Why should I be surprised?" LeBron says. "I was making a lot of great moves. The Pistons are definitely a great defensive team, but I was determined to attack."

When LeBron drives to the bucket, it's best to get out the way. Unless you want to get run over by a 6-foot-8, 240-pound locomotive, that is.

But what makes LeBron so special is his ability to do whatever it takes for his team to be successful. Whether it's handle the ball, pass the ball, rebound the ball, steal the ball, or shoot the ball, King James can do it all.

Come to think of it, LeBron has a game that is probably like your favorite treat. Very sweet.

Don't be afraid to dream big dreams, because with a little luck and a lot of practice, they just might come true.

Just ask Phoenix Suns star guard Steve Nash. Steve grew up in Canada, where he excelled at hockey and soccer at a young age. He didn't begin to play basketball until he was 12 years old. Still, when Steve was in eighth grade, he told his mother that he would be an NBA star one day.

Now that Steve has two Most Valuable Player Awards in his name, it's safe to say that he made good on his promise.

"People have always doubted whether I was good enough to play this game at this level," Steve says. "I thought I was, and I thought I could be. What other people thought was really always irrelevant to me."

Because Canada is known as hockey country, few United States colleges were interested in Steve as a basketball player. He accepted a scholarship to attend Santa Clara, a smaller school located near San Francisco. There he led the Broncos to three trips to the NCAA Tournament and piled up more assists than anyone in school history.

"It seems like my whole life that I've been this little Canadian kid dreaming somebody would give me a chance," Steve says.

Steve was the 15th pick of the 1996 NBA draft, but he couldn't crack the Suns' lineup and was traded to the Dallas Mavericks two years later. The 6'3", 178-pounder started to figure out the pro game, and no player has been more valuable the last few years.

Along with close buddy Dirk Nowitzki, Steve led the Mavericks to the 2002 Western Conference finals. Rather than match their offer for him, the Mavericks allowed Steve to return to the Suns two years later.

Not only is Steve one of the best passers in the game, but he can shoot the ball, too. He is one of only four NBA players to sink more than 50 percent of his field goal tries, 40 percent of his three-pointers, and 90 percent of his free throws in one season.

Even though Steve has achieved success, he will continue to dream big dreams.

"I was never supposed to play in college—let alone the NBA," Steve says. "So I always feel like I have something to prove."

When the sun shines and the wind is at your back, it's easy to laugh and be happy.

But as star forward Dirk Nowitzki (pronounced No-VIT-ski) knows, you can tell a lot more about a person when the rain dumps on his head and the wind blows in his face.

In the 2006–2007 regular season, Dirk and the Dallas Mavericks could almost do no wrong. The team won 67 games in the regular season, more than any other in the league. Dirk averaged 24.6 points and 8.9 rebounds per game. He received the Most Valuable Player trophy.

"Winning 60 games is a special season," Dirk points out.

Then the playoffs started.

In the first round, the Mavericks squared off against the Golden State Warriors, one of the few teams that had given them trouble in the regular season. Before Dirk and the Mavericks knew what had happened, the Warriors beat them four times in five games. *Poof!* The dream of an NBA championship disappeared right before their eyes.

As one might expect, Dirk felt pretty low for several weeks. Finally, rather than allow the bad memory to ruin his summer, Dirk took a vacation in Australia, where he forgot about basketball and remembered the good things in life.

"At some point, you got to get over it and look forward," says Dirk. "You can't just always look at the negative."

Dirk was born in Germany, where his mother and father were excellent handball players. As a teenager, he started to be noticed for his basketball skills.

Years later, Dirk is one of the most talented big men in the game. The 7-footer is a dead-eye from the outside, where he launches shots over smaller opponents with ease. He rarely misses at the free throw line.

At 30 years old, Dirk has plenty of time to climb the mountain again, and if he does reach the top of it, he will be a stronger person when he gets there.

Tony Parker is one of the best point guards in basketball. He plays for the San Antonio Spurs, one of the best teams. He is married to Eva Longoria, a well-known actress who was named by *People* magazine as one of the 50 most beautiful people in the world.

Geez, is Tony a lucky guy or what?

But when you realize what Tony has done to get where he is today, then you have to admire him, rather than be jealous of him.

Born in Belgium and raised in France, Tony is at his best when he

hotfoots it to the basket. He is so quick and such a good ball-handler that it's easier to catch a live fish with bare hands than to corner him. The man called "T.P." scores many of his points on layups or floaters that bank off the backboard.

But guards also have to shoot the ball well from the outside to be complete players. When Tony came into the league, his shooting needed a lot of work. So he had a decision to make: Was he happy just to be a good player, or did he want to become a great one?

Rather than take the summer off, Tony worked with a coach to improve his shot after the 2004–2005 season. He moved the position of his thumb on the ball. He forgot about three-pointers and concentrated on shots closer to the basket. Tony practiced a lot, doing a few hundred jump

shots almost every day—which means a few thousand jump shots almost every week!

When the next season began, Tony was an even better player. He averaged 18.9 points per game, sank more than half of his field goal tries, and was invited to the All-Star Game for the first time.

"It's a nice reward for all the hard work I put in," says Tony, a big fan of video games, Michael Jordan, and mac 'n' cheese. "I'm proud."

For Tony, 2006–2007 was a dream season. He played in the All-Star Game once again. A few months later, in the NBA Finals, T.P. averaged 24.5 points per game. He was selected Most Valuable Player and was the first European-born player to receive the award.

A few days later, Eva and Tony were married in a castle near Paris.

Says Tony, "2007 is a year that I will remember for the rest of my life."

Every so often, the baton is passed to the next great player when he is ready and able to take over as the best at his position.

For the position of point guard, Magic Johnson passed it off to John Stockton, who passed it to Jason Kidd, who passed it to Steve Nash, who will have to give it up himself one day. . . .

And it looks like Chris Paul is almost ready to take it.

In his first two seasons, Chris was one of the best passers and ball-

handlers in the league. But last season was the first that the New Orleans Hornets' floor leader became a threat to score 20 points every game.

Just as Chris raised his performance to another level, the Hornets became one of the most improved teams in the league. Whenever there was talk about the Most Valuable Player Award around the league, Chris was one of the first players to be mentioned.

"I'm just a little bit more confident," explains Chris, who is only 23 years old. "Just sort of knowing where my shots are going to come from. Just understanding the game more and more. A lot of things are coming easier now."

Whenever Chris has a basketball in his hands, things come naturally for him, it seems.

In high school, Chris was a star at West Forsyth High School in North Carolina. In 2003, as a senior, he averaged 30.8 points per game and led his team to a 27–3 record. It was no surprise that Chris was named Mr. Basketball in the state.

Chris attended college at Wake Forest, which was close to his home. In his two seasons there, his team, the Demon Deacons, was invited to the NCAA Tournaments twice and advanced to the Sweet Sixteen once. Even though he was only at the school for two years, Chris is still one of the leaders in points, assists, and steals in Wake Forest's history.

In the 2005 NBA Draft, the Hornets selected Chris at the fourth pick. In his first season, he led all rookies in points, assists, and steals. He was selected T-Mobile Rookie of the Year as a result.

Now that his offense matches the other parts of his game, it's scary to think how good Chris could be in the years to come.

Tim Duncan is a rather quiet giant, but the San Antonio Spurs star doesn't need to say much, really. It takes the 6'11" forward only a few words to say a lot.

"Good, better, best, never let it rest until your good is better and your better is best," Tim likes to say.

Those are the words that Tim has lived by throughout his career.

Born in the Virgin Islands, Tim got off to a late start in basketball and didn't play seriously until ninth grade. He made up for lost time quickly, though. An All-American at Wake Forest where he attended college, Tim was good enough to be the first pick in the 1997 NBA Draft.

Before Tim came aboard, the Spurs were one of the worst teams around. But along with center David Robinson, he carried them to the playoffs and received the Rookie of the Year Award for his efforts. One season later, they led San Antonio to the first NBA championship in Spurs history.

As Tim worked hard on his game and gained more experience, his good got better.

In the 2001–2002 season, the best of his career, Tim averaged 25.5 points, 12.7 rebounds, and 2.5 blocked shots per game. He had more field goals, free throws, and rebounds than any player in the league. That year Tim was selected Most Valuable Player for the first time.

One season later, the Spurs won it all again. And Tim was selected MVP one more time.

"I am the leader of this team," says Tim, who likes to take bank shots on the court and play video games off of it. "So it starts with me, and I understand that."

True to his words, Tim wouldn't let it rest even then.

The Spurs captured their third league crown in the 2004–2005 season. And like he was in the 1999 and 2003 NBA Finals, Tim was handed the MVP trophy once again.

Good, better, best, never let it rest until your good is better and your better is best.